Let's Be Animals

by Ann Turner • pictures by Rick Brown

HarperFestival®
A Division of HarperCollins*Publishers*

Let's be animals,
you and me.

We can baaa and bark and hop.
We can moo and clippity-clop.

I can be a cat
with whiskers I can twirl,
and a tail to loop and curl.

Meow! Meow! Meow!

You can be a dog
with spotted paws of brown,
and a mouth that never frowns.

Woof! Woof! Woof!

I can be a rabbit
with a gray and twitchy nose,
and long fur-covered toes.

Hop!

Hop! Hop!

You can be a sheep
with a coat that looks like snow
to keep off winds that blow.

Baaa! Baaa! Baaa!

I can be a pig
with a pink and pudgy snout
to dig the acorns out.

Oink! Oink! Oink!

You can be a horse
with hooves that clippity-clop,
and never, ever stop.

Neigh! Neigh! Neigh!

I can be a calf
with little pointed horns
to butt my pail of corn.

Moo!
Moo!
Moo!

You can be a goose
with wings of white and gray
to fold at end of day.

Honk!
Honk!
Honk!

There's so much we can be,
you and me,
a mouse or a goat or a hen.